CHARL
COMES TO TOWN

Written by Diane C. Ohanesian
Illustrated by Mike Smollin

Charlie was a happy little train. He loved going up, down, and all around the countryside.

One day, there was an emergency in the nearby town. One of the enormous trains that went to the city broke down. Another train would have to fill in. They needed Charlie!

Charlie was so proud!

"Being a big city train will be so exciting," he thought. He was happy, even though he would miss the green and quiet countryside.

It was Charlie's first day in the city. It was scary. . . so many tracks and trains and signals and sounds. Charlie looked up at the proud, shiny engines. They seemed like giants to him.

The big trains ran right past Charlie. They tooted their deep loud whistles at him as they raced by. "Can't you move any faster?" their whistles seemed to shout at Charlie. That made him feel very sad.

He heard loud laughter.

"Look at the tiny train they sent to help us," tooted one of the big engines. "What can he do?" The other trains started to laugh, too.

"I'll show them," Charlie thought. "I'm going to be the best train they ever saw around here, even if I am little!" He worked very hard, but it wasn't easy. All those stations and signs and signals! There was so much to try to remember!

Charlie was always late getting to work and always late getting back.

"You're just a little country train," said one of the big engines. "You'll never be a real city train."

Watch those signals, Charlie! Charlie tried to remember what all the blinking lights were for, but the poor little train got so confused.

"What's the matter, Charlie? Can't you read the signals?" the big trains tooted and hooted as they roared by.

Charlie was trying to be a good city train, but he was sad and lonely. The other trains weren't friendly. The work was hard. He wondered if he really belonged in the city after all.

One night there was a terrible rainstorm. Charlie sat in the station and cried tears that were as big as the biggest raindrops.

"Maybe those city trains are right," he thought. "I can't run as fast as they can or read the signals as quickly as they do. Maybe I'd better go back to the country."

The next morning, the sun was shining again, but there was trouble on the railroad! The big storm had washed away a whole section of the track. All of the trains had come to a stop to see what could be done.

There was only one way to get through. The trains would have to go up, down, and all around the tracks that went through the nearby hills.

"This won't be a problem for me," roared the biggest engine, tooting its deep, loud whistle and starting its powerful engine. Its big wheels started to move.

The train moved a little way along the track, but it was too big and clumsy to swing and turn on the curving track. It tried and tried, but at last it had to roll back.

Then all the other powerful engines tried to pull their trains along the track. But not even the strongest ones could stay on.

Finally, it was Charlie's turn. He tooted his whistle and off he went. Hurray for Charlie! He went up, down, and all around the shiny track just as if it were his country route. He made all the curves, stopped at all the stops, and tooted all the way into the city.

The big trains could hardly believe their eyes! They stood there as Charlie tooted and whistled his way along the tracks.

Now Charlie was busy all day long. The big trains were parked behind the station. Only Charlie could get to the city while the track was being repaired.

"I guess we were wrong about Charlie," admitted one of the big engines. "He isn't only a little country train after all."

When the track was ready again, all the big trains lined up and gave a big toot-toot salute. Then they put Charlie at the head of the line so he could lead them all into the city. Charlie felt so proud!

When it was time to go back to the country, Charlie was sad to leave his new city friends. But as he went up, down, and all around the countryside, he remembered what they had said. He was a good country train and a good city train too.